# eric

Tundra Books, an imprint of Penguin Random House Canada Young Readers,
a division of Penguin Random House of Canada Limited

Library and Archives Canada Cataloguing in Publication

Title: Eric / Shaun Tan.

Names: Tan, Shaun, author.

Identifiers: Canadiana (print) 20200174797 | Canadiana (ebook) 20200174819 |
ISBN 9780735269736 (hardcover) | ISBN 9780735269743 (EPUB)

Subjects: LCGFT: Picture books.

Classification: LCC PZ7.1.T36 Er 2020 | DDC j823/.92—dc23

Book design by Shaun Tan, Inari Kiuru & Phil Falco

The artwork in this book was created using graphite
and colored pencil on paper.
The text was set in Bodoni.

Printed and bound in China

www.penguinrandomhouse.ca

1   2   3   4   5      24   23   22   21   20

Penguin
Random House
tundra   TUNDRA BOOKS

ERic
by Shaun Tan

**some years ago** we had a foreign exchange student come to live with us. We found it very difficult to pronounce his name correctly, but he didn't mind. He told us to just call him "Eric."

We had repainted the spare room, bought new rugs and furniture
and generally made sure everything would be comfortable
for him. So I can't say why it was that Eric chose to sleep and
study most of the time in our kitchen pantry.

"It must be a cultural thing," said Mum.
"As long as he is happy."

We started storing food and kitchen things in other
cupboards so we wouldn't disturb him.

But sometimes I wondered if Eric *was* happy;
he was so polite that I'm not sure he would have
told us if something bothered him.

A few times I saw him through the pantry door gap,
studying with silent intensity, and imagined what it
might be like for him here in our country.

Secretly I had been looking forward to having a
foreign visitor – I had so many things to show him.
For once I could be a local expert, a fountain of
interesting facts and opinions. Fortunately, Eric was very
curious and always had plenty of questions.

Unfortunately, they weren't the kind of questions
I had been expecting. Most of the time I could only say,
"I'm not really sure," or "That's just how it is."
I didn't feel very helpful at all.

I had planned for us to go on a number of weekly excursions together, as I was determined to show our visitor the best places in the city and its surroundings.

I think Eric enjoyed these trips,
but it was hard to really know.
He just didn't say very much.

Most of the time he seemed only interested in
small things he discovered on the ground.
I might have found this a little exasperating,
but I kept thinking about what Mum had said.

About the cultural thing.

Then I didn't mind so much.

Even so, none of us could help but be
bewildered by the way Eric left
our home: a sudden departure early
one morning, with little more than
a wave and a polite goodbye.

It actually took us a while to realize
he wasn't coming back.

There was much speculation
over dinner later that evening.
Did Eric seem upset?
Did he enjoy his stay?
Would we ever hear from him again?

An uncomfortable feeling hung in the air,
like something unfinished, unresolved.
It bothered us for hours, or at least until one
of us discovered what was in the pantry.

Go and see for yourself.
It's still there after all these years, thriving in
the darkness. It's the first thing we show any
new visitors to our house.
"Look at what our foreign exchange student
left for us," we tell them.

"It must be a cultural thing," says Mum.

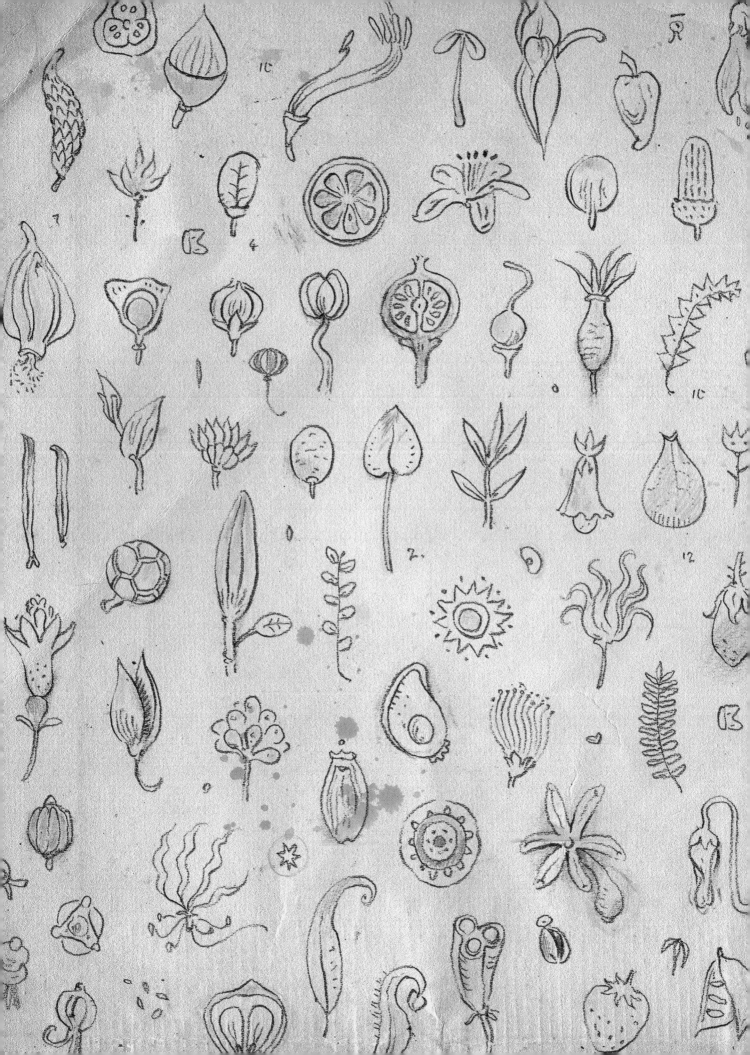